CW00854548

Gentle George

by
Ken Mackenzie and Chris Stead

Written by: Ken Mackenzie and Chris Stead
Editing by: Chris Stead
Design by: Old Mate Media
Illustrations by: Sm-Arts
Cover Art by: Vijesh Valsalan

Published by: Old Mate Media
Any queries to: books@oldmatemedia.com

FIRST EDITION

Print ISBN: 978-1-925638-75-2
Digital ISBN: 978-1-925638-76-9

WWW.OLDMATEMEDIA.COM

Dedication

For all those who worked and continue
to work underground.

CHAPTER 1

Grubb's Coal Mine

There's a little isle off the western edge of Europe called England; you must have heard of it? It's quite famous, you know.

If you head into the middle of England there is another famous place called Yorkshire. And in the hills of Yorkshire there's a little village called Grubbtown. Strange name isn't it?

Now, next to this village you will find a little stream that winds its way down to the valley from the top of the highest hill in the surrounding range. And next to that stream there is a cave that leads deep underground. That's where you'll find Grubb's Coal Mine.

Grubb's Coal Mine is a mysterious place. It's so deep that no sunlight had ever reached the bottom. It's always cold, dark and very, very wet.

Every day most of the men and some of the boys from the village would walk up the hill to the entrance to the mine. They would

then make the long dark journey down the shaft to the bottom.

If they were lucky, they could fit into the one lift that took miners straight to the lowest tunnel.

But it took too long and couldn't hold many people. As such, most miners had to use a long ramp that spiralled down into the earth, going around and around and getting deeper all the time.

The men and boys then spent the whole day digging the coal out from the rock and dirt with shovels and axes. This way, the people around England could put it on their fires.

As they dug, the tunnels in the mine got longer and longer. So, they had to use wood to build a brace every few metres to stop the tunnels from collapsing.

Then they dig long chimneys from the surface all the way down to the tunnels so that air could get in. Having air all the way down at the bottom of Grubb's Coal Mine is very important. Miners are people just like you and I; which means miners need to breathe, too.

It was scary and dangerous work, make no mistake; even for the men. But think about the pit boys. Pit boys were the youngest miners of all who went straight into the mines after finishing school. Some of them were as young as 12; can you believe that!?

At the end of each long day, the miners would have to climb all the way back out from the dark to reach the light.

Then, covered head-to-toe in black soot, take weary steps back down to their village for a quick dinner and a long sleep.

Yep, the people of Grubbtown were very tough indeed!

CHAPTER 2

Hard Work

As you can imagine, it was very hard work digging out all that coal. But with no other work available in the village, the boys and their dads had to do it. How else could they afford to buy food for their families and pay their bills?

Now you may be wondering how the men of Grubbtown got all the coal from Grubb's Coal Mine to the surface so it could be sold? Good on you for asking, because the answer is very interesting.

Down in the dark depths of the mine, the miners put all the coal into big iron bins. The bins were far too heavy for the men to move, so they used little horses called pit ponies to pull the heavy coal up to a cave near the surface for them.

Pit ponies are just like regular ponies: they're not unicorns or something magical like that. However, they're called pit ponies because they work in the pits. Which is another way of saying mines.

So, these pit ponies worked all day pulling the big iron bins from the furthest, darkest tunnel up towards the cave. And if you thought mining coal all day was tough work, well, try pulling huge iron bins full of rock!

These pit ponies did the hardest work of all, but they didn't get to go home to warm beds and full tables of food at the end of the day.

In fact, these pit ponies had never even seen sunshine. They didn't know what it was like to breathe fresh air or run on green grass. That's because they were born in the coal mines and worked all day in the coal mines.

They knew nothing about the outside world. How sad! Those poor old pit ponies.

CHAPTER 3

Meet George

One of the pit ponies was called George. The men who worked in the coal mine called him Gentle George and you'll never guess why. Gentle George was actually the biggest and strongest of all the pit ponies in Grubb's coal mine. Yet he was also the gentlest.

George loved everyone and everyone loved him. And he also worked very, very hard. He'd even help the other pit ponies who weren't as big and strong when they were struggling with their loads or coal.

Sometimes, the men would bring him carrots and George did so love carrots. Sometimes they would also bring him fresh green grass. That was his favourite treat of all. George didn't know what grass was because he had never seen it. But he did know how much he loved eating it.

George's best friend was John, the leader of all the miners. He had a fresh handful of green grass for George every morning. He'd hold it out with one hand, so George didn't

have to eat it off the ground. And
then he'd use his other hand to give
George a big scratch right behind
his ear. It was a fantastic way to start
each day.

CHAPTER 4

The Day It Rained

One day, just before Christmas, the weather was very bad up on the hillside. It was misty, it was raining and it was windy, which is a very unpleasant combination.

As the day went on, the rain got worse and there was no sign of it stopping. This was bad news for the people of Grubbtown in Yorkshire, England. Because rain and mines don't mix.

Eventually the little stream that ran down from the highest hill became a big stream. And then a river. As it filled up with rain the water's edge got higher and higher until it overflowed. All the water then started to run into the cave and down into Grubb's Coal Mine. And the harder it rained, the more water ran into the mine.

But do you think it was raining down in the mines? Of course not! Don't be silly! Deep down underground in the dark, all the men and all the pit ponies were doing their work just as they always do. They had no idea the mine was starting to flood.

That's because the higher tunnels would flood first, not the tunnels right at the bottom. But eventually it got so wet in the high tunnels that the water started to seep through to the tunnels below.

This caused the roof of the mine to start to crumble. The wood braces couldn't hold it up as it turned from solid dirt into slippery mud. Then suddenly, there was a very loud bang and a crashing of rocks and timbers.

The path up to the top of the mine had collapsed. Oh no! Imagine the horror!

CHAPTER 5

Meet John

Unsurprisingly, all the miners and their pit ponies started running. They were all trying to get back to the top of the mine before the passage was blocked by collapsed dirt and high water.

But there were too many men and too many pit ponies down in the

depths of Grubb's Coal Mine and soon they all got stuck trying to be the first into the lift.

It was John, the supervisor, who was in charge. But unfortunately, he had never seen anything like this before. He was very frightened. Actually, it was worse than that; he was terrified! But he also knew it was his job to work out what to do. So, he decided he had to be brave and to make sure that none of the other men could tell how afraid he was.

"What are we going to do?" shouted one of the miners in panic.

John started adding up miners, but soon lost count. There were so many of them working at the bottom of the mine that day. He knew the lift couldn't carry them all to the top before the mine collapsed. Or flooded. Or both!

So, looking down towards the youngest miners in the team, John made the decision.

"The pit boys go first," John bellowed above the panicked voices.

CHAPTER 6

The Pit Boys

John knew the right thing to do was to get the children out first. He ordered the adult miners to get the pit boys into the lift. All the miners stood quietly. They knew their chances of escaping the mine and getting back to the surface were getting worse every second. But they also knew John was right.

"We must send the children first," shouted one man in agreement.

"He's right," hollered another. "Get the boys into the lift."

The men moved aside so all the pit boys could get to the front. They then managed to get all of them squeezed into the lift at once. John pressed the button and slowly the lift started to move and make its way back to the surface, where it was safe.

The men stood and watched as the lift slowly rose up into the dark wet shaft. As they waited, more and more water began to pour down the main shaft. Soon it was ankle deep and rising by the second.

In the distance more and more tunnels could be heard collapsing. And it was getting harder to breathe. John had never been so scared in his entire life.

Suddenly the buzzer sounded on the lift. That sound meant the lift had successfully reached the top. Straight away John pressed the button and the lift started making the slow trip back down to the bottom tunnel.

"The boys are safe," said John. "When the lift gets back, we will go up in groups; six at a time."

The miners sullenly nodded their heads. As the water fell down the shaft, it brought with it the black coal dust that coated all the walls of the mine. Except now that it was wet, it looked like a horrible black sludge, not dust. And soon all the miners were covered in it.

But they had a plan and it was going to work. Or was it? Just as John was in the process of deciding which six men would go first, something terrible happened.

CHAPTER 7

No Lift

S uddenly, there was a loud bang
followed by a rumbling sound just
like thunder. "Get back!" shouted
John as everyone moved deeper into
the tunnel. They only just got out
of the way before the mine lift came
crashing down.

It made such loud noise as it bashed into the ground the noise echoed around the dark tunnel.

Soon after the lift landed a rope came down after it, landing with a splash. It was the rope that was used to pull the lift upwards and lower it down into the mine. All the pit boys must have been too heavy together; it had snapped!

It meant the miners and the pit ponies were trapped

Everyone was quiet for a moment waiting for the echo to die down. Eventually all you could hear was the sound of running water splashing down from the surface above.

Quickly!" said one of the men. "We must try to climb up to the top!"

"It's too high!" said another. "We can't climb that high!"

The pit ponies were very, very frightened by all that crashing and banging. They were used to the wet, but they had never heard or seen anything like this before.

At first, they stood very still and watched everybody running around not knowing what to do. But when the yelling began to echo, they got spooked. The pit ponies reared up onto their back legs in fright, then ran away as fast as they could deeper into the mines.

All except Gentle George.

CHAPTER 8

The Biggest
And The
Strongest

G entle George didn't know what was happening, but he sensed there was danger. So, he stood his ground and stayed with the men that were trapped.

The lamps that provided light in the mine started to run out of fuel or get too wet to keep burning. One by one they flickered out until there were just a few left offering very little visibility. It became very, very dark and the only sound was the dripping of water and the splashing of feet as scared men ran about in circles.

"What can we do?" said one of the men. "How will we make our way back to the top?"

George could see how worried the miners were, but he was just a pit pony, so what could he do? He slowly walked over to where the men were

standing. He stood next to John and lowered his head into John's hand.

"Good boy." said John, scratching behind his ear. "Somehow we will get out of here."

But George didn't walk over for a scratch. George had an idea. He lowered his head into the black muddy water and picked up the end of the piece of rope.

"That's it!" shouted John. "The pit ponies! If we tie the rope to them, they can pull the lift to the top."

"But they've all run away!" said one of the men. "There's only George left, and he could never pull all of us and the heavy lift right up to the surface. It's too far!"

John put his hand on George's back. "What do you think George? Could you pull that much weight?"

George looked him in the eye and gave a big whinny. Of course, George didn't know what John had said as horses don't speak like people. But they were good friends. George knew what John wanted him to do.

And he believed he could do it.

CHAPTER 9

An Almighty Pull

"It's our only chance," said John as the other miners gathered around. "I'll tie the rope around George's shoulders."

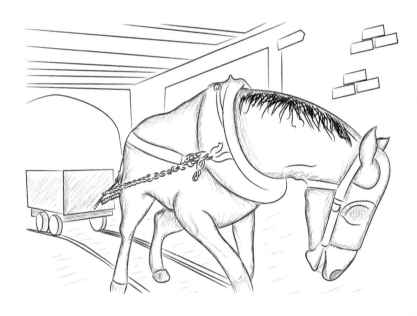

40

"Now George," whispered John into his friend's ear. "You must pull with all your might. You must keep going until we reach the top. You are our only chance!"

John asked the first six men to gather on the broken floor of the lift. He then got the rope and looped it back around the pulley, before tying a loop in the end and placing it over George's neck. He pushed it down so it was sitting around his broad chest and wouldn't choke him.

Then the men all shouted together, "Go George, go! Pull! Pull! Pull with all your strength!"

George started to pull, but the lift was so heavy. It barely even got off the ground at first.

"Pull!" shouted the men again.

So, George summoned all his strength and pulled with all of his might. The lift was so, so heavy. But suddenly it creaked, then it wobbled, and then it started to move. Slowly but surely it started to rise towards the surface.

George began disappearing up a tunnel with the rope wrapped around his chest. His hooves started to slip in the black slime and mud. His legs began sinking deeper and deeper into the floor of the mine with each step. His heart was thumping as the rope around his chest got tighter and tighter. His head was even down so low to the ground that his nose was in the dirty black water.

Twice he almost fell to one knee. And he knew if he fell the rope would yank him all the way back down the tunnel as the lift and its miners fell to ground.

But brave George kept pulling and pulling. It was the hardest thing any pit pony had even been asked to do, but Gentle George would not give up. The men were counting on him.

George had no idea how far he walked up that tunnel pulling the rope, but just when he thought he couldn't possibly take another step from exhaustion, something unexpected happened.

Suddenly, the rope went loose.

CHAPTER 10

A Hero

Gentle George looked back down the tunnel into the dark. He had gone so far; he couldn't see even a hint of John and the other men. Eventually he heard a sound echo up from the dark.

"You've done it!" came John's very excited voice from up the tunnel.

"You're incredible George. You've pulled more than any pit pony has ever pulled before. The men are safe at the top of the mine."

George couldn't believe it. He stood there silently panting and trying to regain his strength. He knew he still had more work to do. Eventually, when he felt up to it, he began slowly walking towards John, lowering the lift back down to the bottom with each step.

As soon as George got to the bottom of the lift John gave him a big hug and the men cheered. But there was no time to waste. The water was already up to knee height and the roof was starting to collapse here and there as it turned all soggy.

"Quick, six more!" John bellowed.

The next six men climbed onto the platform and George knew he had to do it all over again. John stood in front of George, he held George's head in his hands and whispered, "can you do it again old boy? Have you the strength?"

George pricked his ears up, snorted, turned towards the tunnel and lowered his head.

"Pull George, pull!" shouted John. George took a deep breath and pulled. The black sludgy water was getting deeper. It was now halfway up his legs and so cold poor George had started to shake. But slowly the lift began to rise once again as George found the strength.

CHAPTER 11

The Best Of Friends

Back and forth George went. Soon after it was 12 men; then 18 men; then 24 men. George rescued them all. On each trip up the tunnel, the water would be higher; the ground slipperier; the air cooler.

Sometimes he would slip and could feel himself being dragged backwards by the weight of the lift.

But each time George would get up and go again. Ears pricked up and nostrils flared, he'd lunge forward, and the rope would tighten once again around his chest.

George somehow kept finding the strength to pick himself up and take another step. Finally, there was only one person left.

"It's just me now George," John revealed. "You've saved everyone." John climbed onto the ruined lift platform. Exhausted, George slowly raised his head and looked up into John's eyes for the last time.

For a few moments the two stared at each other in silence, before John shook his head.

John jumped down from the platform into the waist deep sludge. He put his hand on George's back and shook his head again. "I can't do it," John said. "I'm not going to leave you on your own George. You and I will get out of here together."

Then both their heads spun around as they heard splashes coming at them down the tunnel. Something was coming from deep down in the mine.

Whatever it was, it was huge, and it was coming right for them!

CHAPTER 12

A Christmas Miracle

George and John stood together looking down the tunnel as the last few lamps flicked down to just tiny flames. Was it some kind of monster? Was it a beast trapped in the depths also trying to escape?

But George quickly recognised the smell and he brayed his delight. The pit ponies that had run off frightened before had returned. However, they didn't bring with them any big ideas on how they might escape.

They were still all trapped, but at least they were trapped together.

Suddenly, there was a big splash as something landed in the water next to the ruined lift. John ran over and yelped for joy. It was a harness, attached to a rope that went all the way up the shaft.

All the men George had rescued had stayed behind at the top of the mine. None of them would leave for Grubbtown until all the pit ponies had been saved.

So, one-by-one, John led the pit ponies to the shaft, put them in the harness and then tugged the rope. The men at the top would then pull the pit pony up to the top and then drop the harness back down.

When it was just George and John again, the miner began fitting the harness around his favourite pony. John wouldn't save himself until he knew his friend had escaped. But he had to hurry; the water was already near John's chin. It wouldn't be long until the mine was fully flooded and John would drown.

When the harness was attached, the men all heaved together and slowly George was pulled up the shaft. As soon as he reached the top, he jumped out of the harness and kicked it back down the shaft to John below. Was he too late? Had the water risen too far?

Thankfully there was a tug on the rope. He was alive! George grabbed the rope in his teeth and pulled John to safety. He came up soaking wet and covered in black sludge, but with a big smile on his face.

Every human and pony was safe.

CHAPTER 13

Sunlight

Gentle George was a true hero, everyone agreed. But his big adventure wasn't over yet. John led him to the edge of the cave and then pulled a big black bag off a shelf and placed it over George's head.

This was not what he expected at all and George started rearing back in panic.

'Don't worry," said John softly. "The rain has stopped outside and the sun is out. The sun is very bright to those who have never seen it before. This black bag will protect your eyes while we lead you to your new home."

George still didn't understand what John was saying, but he knew he could trust his friend.

So, he let John lead him outside the cave, down the hill and past the stream that had become a river. Then as the sun began to set and the sunlight became softer, John removed the bag.

George couldn't believe his eyes. There was fresh, green and oh so yummy grass everywhere. And the air was so clean and crisp. There was a soft breeze on his face and he couldn't see any black coal dust anywhere. All the pit ponies were there, too, looking around in wonder.

Gentle George never had to go into the mine again. He now lives happily in the field with his friends. And every day the men and the pit boys from the village came past to say thank you once more and offer him some treats. And even though they still called him Gentle George, nobody questioned his strength.

Being gentle, it seems, doesn't mean you can't be strong.

The End

ABOUT THE AUTHORS

Ken Mackenzie

Ken Mackenzie is a storyteller. He has always loved reading stories to the younger generation and taking them on a journey to a brighter, kinder world.

Living in Torquay, England, you'll find Ken's music shows transporting listeners in all the hotels and his charity work with the Children's Hospice South West brightening the lives of terminally ill children.

Married to Jill, they have seven beautiful children and twelve amazing grandchildren.

Children's Hospice South West provides care for children who have life-limiting conditions and are not expected to live into adulthood, whilst also supporting their whole family unit.

You can find out more about their essential work if you head to this website; https://www.chsw.org.uk

Old Mate Media is delighted to share that 25% of the profits from the sale of Gentle George will be donated to the Children's Hospice to help them continue their essential work in the community.

Chris Stead

C hris Stead is a prolific children's author with nine children's books and six non-fiction titles published and enjoyed by readers all around the world.

The sense of adventure and imagination that permeates all Chris' work comes from his childhood memories of dreaming about far away worlds and endless possibilities.

He has been writing for far too long, with his first works completed at the age of 11 (still beloved by his parents). Over the years he has presided over multiple award-winning magazines and websites, before turning his skills to publishing.

Now, he lives in Sydney Australia with his wife Kate and three children, Charlie, Jasmine and Patrick.

Writing is still an escape, but it fits in amongst all the trappings of family life, as well as helping authors around the world fulfil their independent publishing dreams.

Share Your Opinion

If you enjoyed George's adventures, we would love you to pop online and leave a review on Amazon or Goodreads. Reviews help other people find and enjoy independent books like ours.

For Amazon:

1. Search "George: The Gentle Giant" in the search bar
2. Click on the book page
3. Scroll down to where it says Customer Reviews
4. Click on Write a Customer Review
5. Note: You'll need to be logged in to your Amazon account.

Goodreads

1. Search "Gentle George" in the search bar
2. Click on the book page that comes up under the search bar
3. Click on the box under the cover image and change to "read"
4. A pop-up box will appear for you to leave a review
5. Once you've typed in your review and left a star rating, you can click on save.

We also love word of mouth, so if your kids loved the book, do let your friends know. They can purchase a book at one of Ken's shows, at local stores in Torquay or on Amazon.

TURN YOUR BOOK DREAMS INTO REALITY

Do you have a story you tell your kids and grandkids all the time? Are your friends and family always telling you, "you should think about becoming an author?"

Old Mate Media is a specialist publishing company that can help you take your creative thoughts from scribblings to a published book. We walk with authors step-by-step along the publishing road, adding our expertise only where it's needed. For free guides and quotes, visit:

www.oldmatemedia.com

READING GOODIES!

Scan the QR Code below to get your free Early Learning and Reading Guide and join our reading community for free books, special bonuses and more.

ALSO BY KEN MACKENZIE

For your younger children, Ken has two lovely picture books available.

You can find both books on Amazon, in Torquay bookstores and directly at Ken's shows.

If you'd like to know when George's second adventure is available, just drop an email to books@oldmatemedia.com and we'll keep you in the loop.

Lightning Source UK Ltd.
Milton Keynes UK
UKHW021106021021
391551UK00011B/183